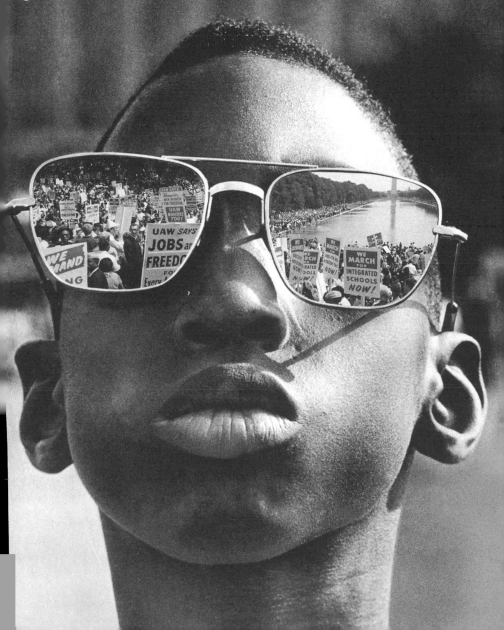

D0283650

VOICES FROM THE MARCH ON WASHINGTON

Poems by
J. Patrick Lewis
&
George Ella Lyon

WORD*S*ONG
AN IMPRINT OF BOYDS MILLS & KANE
New York

To the enduring cause of justice and civil rights

—*JPL*

In gratitude & praise for all who marched
&
in memory of Odetta & Mary Travers

—*GEL*

CONTENTS

ix

INTRODUCTION

I magine a world where everyone at your school, at your church, on your sports team, and in your neighborhood shares the same skin color. Imagine that your box of crayons has a pinkish-beige color called Flesh, but your skin is black or brown. And imagine being barred from restaurants, motels, and stores just because of this. Your parents have no choice in where to live and work, no matter what their qualifications; your school is rundown, your teachers underpaid, your books raggedy—written in, underlined, missing pages, worn out because white students always use them first.

This is how your life would have been if you had been an African American living in the South (and some places in the North) under Jim Crow—the laws that enforced racial segregation—before the civil rights movement; before Rosa Parks kept her seat on an Alabama bus and started the Montgomery Bus Boycott in 1955; before the Freedom Riders were beaten and jailed for their efforts to desegregate transportation in 1961; before that Wednesday in 1963 when 250,000 people came to the March on Washington—the March for Jobs and Freedom—transported by trains, buses, cars, airplanes, bicycles, roller skates, and by their own determined feet.

That day stands out in the civil rights movement because it brought together so many organizations and people from all over the country and abroad, and because it remained peaceful despite the racial tension in the country and the urgent need for change.

First on the March's official list of demands was civil rights legislation "to guarantee all Americans access to all public accommodations, decent housing, adequate and integrated education, [and] the right to vote."

Though the Supreme Court had outlawed segregated schools in 1954 (*Brown vs. Board of Education*), nine years later desegregation was still a slow and sometimes violent process.

In that late summer of 1963, when the Marchers gathered on the Mall, I was a freshman in high school, attending an all-white school in the mountains of Kentucky. My civics teacher did not refer to the civil rights movement in any way; he didn't mention the March or the bombing of the Birmingham church that came soon after; we didn't discuss the sit-ins, the Freedom Riders, the Albany Movement, or the other protests that were happening in the North as well as the South to push for equal rights. Not until President Kennedy was assassinated that November did current events enter our classroom, and they didn't stay long.

But in July 1964, President Johnson signed the Civil Rights Bill that Kennedy had proposed, and that fall our school was desegregated. We had no overt problems, perhaps because coal mining, the heart of our economy, had long been open to African Americans. Sports teams accepted black students because they wanted the best athletes they could get, but there were no girls' sports at that time, and the girls' singing group didn't admit black girls, regardless of how well they sang. The pep club excluded them, too. Desegregation of the classroom was immediate; integration at school took much longer. In the community, it's still underway.

A. Philip Randolph, who founded and ran the first primarily black labor union, the Brotherhood of Sleeping Car Porters, was part of a movement to stage a march on Washington in 1941. At the last minute, that march was called off because President Franklin D. Roosevelt signed an executive order that addressed some of the main concerns of the marchers.

Twenty-two years later, Randolph was determined that this time the March would happen. With the help of John Lewis, Roy Wilkins, James Farmer, Whitney Moore Young Jr., and the Rev. Dr. Martin Luther King Jr.—a group that became known as the "Big Six"—Randolph created a coalition representing students, churches, labor unions, and civil rights organizations. He appointed Bayard Rustin as the March's chief organizer and, on August 28, 1963, he saw all his work come to fruition. He told the quarter-million people in the crowd, "We are the advance guard of a massive, moral revolution for jobs and freedom," and proclaimed that everyone there would "carry the civil rights revolution home."

You may know the March as the occasion for Dr. King's "I Have a Dream" speech, certainly the most dramatic moment of the day, summing up a vision for the future and exhorting all who were present to bring that dream into reality. You may know the March as one of the critical steps leading to the passage of the Civil Rights Act of 1964, which made segregation illegal, and to the Voting Rights Act of 1965, which outlawed discrimination in voting.

But on that sweltering Wednesday half a century ago, no one knew where the steps they were taking would lead. And, crucial as the Big Six were in creating the March and articulating its goals, they were just a tiny island in that multicolored sea of people. Who were the Marchers? Why did they risk their lives to be there? How were they changed by that day?

These are questions we carried in our hearts as we researched and wrote *Voices from the March on Washington*. We hope that in reading our poems, you'll feel as though you're part of that great gathering, with all its idealism and courage. While we've come a long way toward equality in fifty years, we've still got a long way to go. Soon it will be your turn to guide this country. Never forget that you can make a difference. You, too, have a voice.

—*GEL* (with *JPL*)

Note: Various terms (*Negro*, *black*, and *colored*) identify African Americans in this book according to the time period and the documents and quotations in which the words appear.

VOICES FROM THE MARCH ON WASHINGTON

REFLECTION

Lincoln

Great

Emancipator

look out on this day

on its leaders   its speakers   its singers   but most of all

look at its glory, two-hundred and fifty thousand souls come from all corners of this

nation to march for rights you long ago said we had

who are not crushed · by our country's deep
injustice, who still · believe in the dawn
of a better day, who · journeyed here to haul
that sun up. See · this Mall blanketed
with hope, with faith · in spite of fire hoses
belief in freedom · though it lands us
in jail. Reflect · on the hundred
years since you · declared *All persons*
held as slaves shall · *be thenceforward*
and forever free How · can that be true when
Mississippi denies · us the vote? When we
so-called *free* people · in Alabama, Virginia
South Carolina can't · eat, work, live, or learn
anywhere the white · man draws a line?
When the only future · we can give our kids
is the past wearing · different clothes?
This pool is a · mirror revealing
the lie of *separate* · *but equal* that scars
democracy's face · Most of us framing it
struggle at home to · keep our heads above
water and live in fear · if we get too far
above, we might · find a bullet in
our backs. We · gather at this pool
which is full of feet · and sky, full of
promises unfulfilled · but not abandoned

self-evident truths that we are *created equal*   that the wild experiment of *liberty and*

justice for all is still under way   that we can stand

together in our differences   that we are the dream coming true

For All, 1963

If you contend the noblest end
of all is human rights, amend
the laws: The beauty of the sun
is that it shines on everyone.

An Imagined Summit Two Days Before the March

In the hotel room six men, in leatherette chairs
or on the edges of the beds, discuss the March.
The first man, his nerves like plucked strings,
worries that too few people will show up.
"How many are we expecting?" he asks.
"Buses," the second weighs in. "Do we have adequate parking?"
"What about possible violence?" offers the third man.
"How many marshals are in place?" counters the fourth.
The fifth shakes his head, "Can you hear the speakers
if you're a half-mile away from the podium?"
The sixth man jumps in, "And what about enough water?"
The first man's response, "Water, yes, and portable toil—?"
is interrupted by a knock at the door.

The third man opens it.

A hotel guest from next door—a woman in a bathrobe,
mud mask, and curlers—asks, "What on earth could be
so important at two o'clock in the morning?"

This Journey

Some of us go around like we're so smart, we're nothing but a brain
on a stalk. I worked for this day, wrote news releases, sent word to churches,
drove a truck with a loudspeaker to recruit Marchers in DC. I had my checklists,
my two-way radio. Yessir, I was behind this event a hundred percent
but I didn't know what it was about.

Now I stand
in Union Station
and hear Marchers
step down from the trains
singing
Now I watch the weary
climb out of buses
and see hope
rise in their eyes
Now I greet folks arriving
in tobacco wagons
on bicycles

in cars that couldn't make it but did

more Marchers than I dared to imagine

and I feel
my heart surge
my throat clinch with tears
because all of a sudden
I see

This March
didn't grow
from committees
and fundraising and permits

This trip
didn't start yesterday

in Jackson or Tupelo or Boston
or in the march
that didn't happen in 1941

This journey
began with chains in Ghana

We're climbing out of slave castles
up from ships' holds
off of auction blocks
We're climbing
up and out and over
to claim our birthright

and everybody
from the White House and Congress
to the mayor of Itta Bena, Mississippi
better join us or get out
of our way.

How

Myrtle Hill, 60
High School Teacher
Baltimore, MD

I'm dozing when the first rock
hits the bus. Screams and "Lord
have mercy, children!" and "Get down!"
which I do. I hear a window break,
the wall beside me denting in,
feel the bus lurch and pick up speed.

Behind me, Brother Roby's wife, Ada,
starts to sing: *Oh, freedom, oh, freedom* . . .
A busload of voices joins her.
I struggle up. I'm a generous-built
woman, not made for crouching
between bus seats. My heart is
beating so hard, I can barely get
breath to sing, but I manage to join
in on the brand new verse:
No rock throwin', no rock throwin'
No rock throwin' over me, over me . . .
They throw rocks, we throw songs.
DC, here we come.

Among the Marchers

1

Irene Turley, a professional oboist, buttered bread for 80,000
Marchers' cheese sandwiches at New York City's Riverside
Church. Now, as she steps down off the bus in Washington,
she hums a tune, pleased with her small contribution.

2

Quakers in love, Edith and Harry Burlingame,
Fort Lauderdale newlyweds (second time for both),
planned a March-for-Jobs honeymoon. What it takes
is three tanks of gas, motel bedbugs, radiating smiles,
and optimism greater than any other organized religion allows.

3

Everett Goodfellow, amateur birdwatcher, grandson
of a slave, follows Constitution Avenue in the lizard skin
of an old man. After six decades of longing and memory,
Ever's WWI medal is as shiny as his threadbare suit.

4

Working on her PhD thesis—*Race in Langston Hughes's
"The Weary Blues"*—Rebekah Stoddard knows that skin
the color of her own fresh apricot is no ticket to ride.
Not now. Never was.

5

Split-personality man: MosesBenHurCharltonHeston.

6

A Brooklyn band of brethren walks 237 miles to a revolution;
at 82, Jay Hardon rides his bicycle all the way from Dayton, Ohio;
and Ledger Smith roller-skates 750 miles from Chicago,
a streaming red sash trailing in his tail wind—*FREEDOM!*

7

Arthur Howe, a third grader clutching his mother's hand,
sees Negroes and whites laughing together for the first time
in his life, and feels a brace of emotions he cannot reconcile:
confusion and pride.

AGAINST THE MARCHERS

Demon Hate, hiding in the bushes,
a filthy ringside seat,
for one day is wiping from his lips
a bitter brew: defeat.

CROSSING THE POTOMAC

Loretta Turner, 55
Waitress
Oxford, Mississippi

So this is it, huh? When we get to vote,
this is where people we elect will come
to work. This is where cherry
trees bloom in the spring. I've seen
pictures. Where the president closes
his eyes at night. I could not sleep
with that job, no sir. Worry gives me
the Big Eye as it is and I've just got family
and friends and neighbors to worry about.
Well, Mr. Kennedy, we are here to worry
you some more.

                Now this Mall, where
we're all meeting up, I read it was
the Civil War Soldiers' marching ground.
Full of men with their blue suits on, ready
to die to save the Union and set us free.
That's something to tell the grandbabies
about. Tell them, too, their grandma
joined the Civil *Rights* soldiers. Yes, ma'am.
No uniforms just buttons and signs.
No guns. But we've put on that gospel
armor. We'll turn the other cheek like
the Good Lord said, but we have come
for our rights and we won't turn back.

ARRIVAL

All of us are excited. Dr. Hobbs has trained
us in how to act if something goes wrong,
but none of us knows what to expect.

As our bus rolls past the white-columned,
steep-stepped Supreme Court, Hattie Davis
yells, "Go, Justice! We're here to change

the world!" Most of us Spelman women
take up her cry: *Go, Justice! We're here
to change the world! Go, Justice!* . . . I yell,

too, but not as hard as Hattie. We're
here, all right, but change the world? I
don't know. Can that really be done?

Raymond Jarvis, 25
B.A. Degree in Business Administration
Out-of-Work Store Clerk
Amarillo, Texas

The Watch

I watch my business administration degree
    secure a place for me in the unemployment line.

I watch my mother worry that her
    math-star son struggles to earn a living.

I watch the register fill
    till my boss's magic trick makes all
    the "petty cash" disappear.

I watch my paycheck shrink
    ten dollars a week till they fire me
    "for offending a lady in Hardware, boy."

I watch my blister
    of a bungalow get splat-tattooed
    with a red, white, and blue swastika.

I watch the window
    and the rock sailing through the window
    with a promise.

I watch the moon
    as if the moon had any answers,
    her face hidden in a disgrace of clouds.

I watch my no-account savings account
    buy a cup of coffee and a heap of humiliation,
    and you ask me why I'm going to the March?

IOWAYS

Superstitions in Seymour, Iowa
are stranger than a cloud of gnats
in a hatbox. Like: The sun glows
golden because it's staring down
at the mirror of our sweet Ioway
corn, piglets are God's own puppies,
and combines and tractors won't
run proper without nicknames—
John-John Dear, Cutterpillar.
Growing up snow-white in this
snow-white land, any farm girl
capable of plumb-bob thought
could get a hankering to BB
the blue jays off the hay bales.

In the secret language of family,
Seymour equaled Home, crib-to-casket.
So the invisible cinch that pinched
and sheep-shanked me to the porch
stretched for five generations of Wallaces.

A country of mystery lay beyond
the books that motored my imagination.

THE REAL QUESTION

I'm a college student in Virginia,
a state practicing Massive Resistance
to school integration. Prince Edward
County has no public school at all
this fall. So my friends and I see
the March as our chance to make
a public statement against that shame,
to move toward something right.

Yesterday we drove to my parents' house
in DC. This morning we made a sign:
"William and Mary supports the March
on Washington," which the college
absolutely does not. But for today
we *are* the college, see? *We* become
its conscience. As we leave the house
my kid sister asks, "Why are you going?"
"It's time," my buddy says.

"Why are you staying?"

BUT THEY DID

found in
Bayard Rustin: Troubles I've Seen
by Jervis Anderson

"How," asked a writer
for the *National Guardian*,
"do you move [that] many people
into a crowded, unfamiliar city
—by rail, bus, plane, and private car—
making certain that they arrive
no earlier than 6 a.m.
and no later than 10 a.m.?
What do you do with them
once they have arrived?
How do you feed the hungry,
refresh the thirsty, care for the sick,
discipline the undisciplined?
How do you make certain
that all these people get back
on their buses at precisely 5:30 p.m.,
so that they leave the city by nightfall?"

An official of Washington's police
department was just as doubtful.
"I don't see how they're going
to make it," he said.

BAYARD RUSTIN

A wizard of fox-wit and tiger-will
lived on an island called Invincible.
He was asked if, in two months' time,
he could brew a city into a stew of a quarter-
million people. A disgusting word flickered in
his brain, climbed the wall, ran through the streets.
It would not let him go. Even in his dreams,
the word assailed him, till he woke to see it
suspended menacingly in the air.
He reached out and grabbed it.

Impossible

The wizard lit a candle, snuffed out
the word, chuckled to himself,
and set to work on the city stew.

DAN CANTRELL, 16
RABUN COUNTY HIGH SCHOOL JUNIOR
DILLARD, GEORGIA

MOTIVATION

"Don't you go," Dad said.
"Don't you dare go to that march."

That's not what got me here,
but it helped.

EMMA WALLACE, 23
FARM HAND
SEYMOUR, IOWA

MY PA

I came hungry
into the world,
and for that,
look no further
than my Pa.
A history buff
and a small-*p*
poet, he built
so many book-
shelves, our house
became the local
lending library.
At least to those few
who knew a book
to be a friend.

BREAKFAST

I don't remember the bus pulling up.
I don't remember getting off, either.
Daddy must have carried me

to this grassy place where he sets
me down under a tree. He takes
a parcel out of his jacket pocket,

unwraps a ham biscuit and hands
it to me. I just hold it, looking up
at him fine against the blue sky.

Then he bends close and says,
"Your mama made that, Ruby May."
Still I hold back. Too much *strange*

all around. Daddy takes my biscuit back,
makes it open and close like a mouth,
says, "Better bite it before it bites you!"

I giggle and eat. Home tastes so good.

RAYMOND JARVIS, 25
B.A. DEGREE IN BUSINESS ADMINISTRATION
OUT-OF-WORK STORE CLERK
AMARILLO, TEXAS

THE RIDE

When we take our seats, the bus comes alive,
honeybee people swarming to a hive,
buzzing with excitement and disbelief
at doing *something* to ease our grief.

Yells the driver, "It's thirty hours or more
before we reach what y'all are shouting for."
My cousin taps me from across the aisle,
"I'm betting on us every Greyhound mile.

If this bus is aimed at the Promised Land,
they won't be promises built on sand."
I nod off, sleeping most of the way,
dreaming of a Raymond future someday.

GLORY AND DESPAIR

"Who knew there were this many Negroes?"
Ty Tucker whined to three
of his four-man Horse Police Patrol
in the shade of a linden tree.

Apache stamped his hoof and nickered,
Glory champed at the bit.
Tall in the stirrups, Tucker laughed.
"It's a barbecue benefit."

A grandmother and child looked on,
cautiously standing clear
of animals that snuffled, stood
and stared, and showed no fear.

But seeing awe in her child's eyes,
the woman said, "Could my
little grandson pet your horses, sir?"
"Keep movin', girl," growled Ty.

The boy tried hard to love the March,
but standing in the way
was the angry man on the pretty horse
that happened to him that day.

Dan Cantrell, 16
Rabun County High School Junior
Dillard, Georgia

HITCHING

I've just stuck out my thumb
and held up my **DC or BUST**
sign when Matt Osage's dad
pulls over and opens his door
saying, "I can take you
as far as Berea, Kentucky."

It's twilight when Mr. Osage
lets me off in hilly country a lot
like home, so I am surprised
when, after three cars dust
me, a blue pickup stops.
A skinny woman in faded
jeans and a red bandana shirt
says her name is Judy Gilley.
I tell her I'm headed to DC
for the March. She says
she's driving to Ripley,
West Virginia, to see her sister
through surgery. She's happy
to carry me that far if I will

just sign in. I dig for some
manners. "Pardon?" I ask.
"Guest book in the glove box,"
she tells me. "Name, address,
phone number, destination.
Oh—and your age."

"Yes, ma'am," I say.
I climb in and get settled,
duffel and all, then push
the silver button and take
out a white, plastic-covered
book. It needs that plastic.
Some pages, dented with
smudgy scrawl, show
thumbprints. At the end
of the list, I add the facts
of me, plus *Thank you*.
"Put the date, too, please,"
she says. "Helps my recall."

I write it bold: *August
26, 1963*. Then I have to
ask, "Aren't you afraid
to pick up strangers?"

"I've got your name,"
she says. "But you don't
know it's my name," I
tell her. "And you don't
know mine is Judy Gilley,"

she points out. She sort
of has me there. "Besides,"
she goes on, "I don't stop
for everybody. One day I
saw a man and two women
out by Paint Lick Creek.
Gave me a funny feeling,
and I drove on by. Turned
out they'd just buried
a body in the woods. So, see?
I'm careful." We laugh.

I'm careful, too. I'm never
telling my parents about this!

THE BLIND LEADING . . .

I wouldn't be here at all except for my sister Josephine
who is blind. I've been in jail in Albany where Georgia
police took the blackjack to my back. I didn't plan
on traveling eight hundred miles to get my head bloodied
too. You got to understand what we've been through
this summer—cattle prods and Medgar Evers gunned down.
This country is a dynamite box. I think if *any* violence breaks
out at this March, our next stop could be the Pearly Gates.

To say I don't feel protected by the government is to say
trees have leaves. I'm a history major and I learned a thing
or two about protest before I got myself hauled into jail.
I know the United States government sent bombers to intimidate
miners in West Virginia in 1921—and most of those men were
only black from coal dust. I know in 1932 they sent tanks against
World War I vets who came to DC to collect their bonuses.

So I know if the March draws the crowd we want and things go
bad, DC police and soldiers will make Albany look like a picnic.
Then why am I here? Because Josephine said, "You think our
rights are going to be won in Georgia? No, ma'am. If we
want change, we've got to go to Washington and show them
numbers. I may be blind, but you're the one can't see."

LENA

Lena Horne, 46
Internationally Famous
Singer and Actress

Instead
Of her
        Most famous song,
"Stormy
Weather,"
        She sang one long,

Strong word,
"Free-*eeee*-dommmm!"
        And that would be
One fine
Eight-second
        Symphony.

RAYMOND JARVIS, 25
B.A. DEGREE IN BUSINESS ADMINISTRATION
OUT-OF-WORK STORE CLERK
AMARILLO, TEXAS

MY DREAM

The March should strike and poke and prod,
like a lightning rod,

walk, then run—wild
as the wonder of a child.

The March should measure its success
by the white man's distress.

To leave a legacy behind—
unpeace of mind—

the March should spark a million candle-watts
of afterthoughts.

The March should welcome every guest
who's dispossessed,

and search, with map, flashlight, and key,
for our humanity.

To all imaginations out of whack or work,
college grad and filing clerk,

panhandler and politician,
the March, if it's to meet its mission,

must stand against evils, present and past,
God Almighty, at long last.

GRACE

Mama said,
"The one
who stands out
is the one
who dies."

Daddy said,
"Might as well
try on
a noose
for size."

My brother said,
"Think
of your future!
Stick
to your place."

My sister said,
"Hallelujah!
I'll go
with you,
Grace."

"MOVEMENT"

Did I first hear that word
in a dream? Was it the true
coin of my father's realm?
Reckless talk spelled
misdemeanor money in
our county, but "movement"
snuck into the pages
of a newspaper, spilled
over me and stuck.

One day, out in the barn,
I said, "Lately, Pa,
I've been thinking
about all the people
and places I don't even
know I don't even know."

"Destiny's waiting for you,
darlin'," he said. "Close
to a thousand miles

beyond the last stoplight,
about five states over,
that national powwow
you've been jawing about
will surely shame the past
and shape the future.
You'd best get started,
Em, before corn tassels
lasso and thrash every
last one of your dreams."

HALLEY LIZA CLEMONS

30, Hotel Maid
Nashville, Tennessee

A pause between speakers
and a man white as a pillowslip

asks where I came from,
how I got here. I say

Nashville, Tennessee. I took
a bus. That satisfies him.

He's from Kentucky. He drove.

But it would be truer to say
somebody sang me here.

If it wasn't for some old
woman, one of my greats,

humming, working
dark to dark, never giving

up, I wouldn't even *be*. She
kept the song of our blood

going. She carried me here.

TOKEN

Fifth on the program—
A Tribute to Negro Women Fighters for Freedom.
Listed are:

Diane Nash Bevel
Rosa Parks
Gloria Richardson
Daisy Bates
Mrs. Herbert Lee
Mrs. Medgar Evers

One led the effort to desegregate Nashville lunch counters.
Another refused to get up from the white section of the bus.
One marched for equal housing and hospitals.
Another conducted the Little Rock Nine into school
despite a threat thrown through her window:
Stone this time. Dynamite Next.
Two saw the threats made real,
their husbands murdered, martyred.

We wouldn't let them march on the same street as us
but we decided to let one speak.

DOUBTS

"You must be suffering from heat stroke,"
Mama said, "to think parades work miracles."

"Audrey," Daddy said, "will you show a little
respect for your daughter? Renée's done a lot
of thinking about it, and she's going!"

Right there I wanted to jump in and say
I was just respecting Daddy's wishes,
but shut my mouth—I had the confidence
of a toad at a frog reunion.

Can a look be both hopeful and hopeless
at the same time? That's the pitiful way
Daddy stared at me. Maybe he knew more
than I did. For once. Which wouldn't be
hard since I knew so little about the March
that promised to be a policemen's ball,
especially if Grandma Rascal—
the nickname fits!—was joining us.

So guess where the three of us are going
tomorrow. That's why I spent Tuesday
afternoon writing this list. . . .

Renée Newsome, 15
Coolidge High School Sophomore
Washington, DC

Things to Do at the March

1. Pack my *Selected Poems of Langston Hughes*.
2. Take my diary. Somebody might say something interesting?
3. Look for Darryl, in case he decides to march after all.
4. Buck up the courage to meet 3 new people.
5. Mingle.
5. (repeat) *Try* to mingle!
6. Help Daddy carry his beautiful homemade poster—
    WE ARE ALL JACKIE
    ROBINSONS TODAY
7. "Watch—Listen—Roar!" (Grandma Rascal's motto, though I'm not sure what good it will do.)
8. Show Mama her heat-stroke daughter can tell a miracle from just any old street parade.
9. Let doubt about the March fight it out against hope for its success. See who wins.
10. Hide Grandma's bullhorn.

DAN CANTRELL, 16
RABUN COUNTY HIGH SCHOOL JUNIOR
DILLARD, GEORGIA

AT THE WASHINGTON MONUMENT

I couldn't explain
to my mom and dad why I
had to be here, why

home had gotten too
small. Dad was always laying
down the law and I

never got a vote.
Marching for jobs and freedom
sounded good to me.

I needed both. Truth
to tell, I hadn't thought much
about race—hadn't

had to, though I cringed
every time Dad got on a
drunken rant about

Negroes. The March pulled
me north the way November
pulls birds south: time to

wing it, go where you've
never been. Sky gets loud and
full of their journey

like the Mall this DC
morning, where I make my way,
hungry and groggy,

among more folks than I've ever seen.

WATCHING

One reason Daddy brought me
and not Jeanette, who's seven,
is that I'm not a wiggle-worm.
Mama says I could sit through
church even if it went from
the manger to the stone rolled
away. I like the singing and I
like to watch folks when they
do things they don't think
you see. Like that boy whose hair
was long as the girl's he was kissing
behind their sign. Like the woman
whose guitar string broke and flew
up and hit her on the cheek—how
she threw back her head and just
sang louder, how she was dark
as me and full of beautiful.

"M"

Charlie Jackson, 39
Detective
Jersey City, New Jersey

I am nothing out of the ordinary,
a Jersey City detective wired
to an ordinary life. Wearing an "M" for marshal
and my white Gandhi hat, I'm standing
by the great Dr. King himself.
For a few hours, I feel . . . extraordinary.

The fear of violence vs. the violence of fear.
Neither one wins. They lock up every bar
in the city; the strongest drink on tap is lemonade.
Washington Senators baseball: postponed.
Hear the young Negro men with walkie-talkies?
They've trained for weeks in crowd control:
"Freedom Two to Equality One,"
"Jobs Four to Justice Two."

I'm lucky I met Hank Aaron, Muhammad Ali,
and Ossie Davis, but the Reverend outshines
them all. I gaze up at the sky during The Speech:
Two clouds meet to form a cross. I'd bet my badge
it's a sign from God that sets Dr. King's words ablaze.

Emma Wallace, 23
Farm Hand
Seymour, Iowa

My Own Particular Heart

Now I'd wager I hadn't seen
an actual Negro but a dozen times
in my neighborhood. An innocent
as white as baby turnips but bent
on grace and growth of the mind,
I wanted to meet folks who manage
every day to survive hammers of hate,
facing obstacles light-years beyond
my pitiful pocketbook of complaints.

I wanted to slap at spider webs
thick enough to shut out the sun
and find the tucked-away bits
of Emma Wallace. Which is why I
listened to the music of a particular heart—
my own at 23—and how I came to jump
gingerly off a Burlington Trailways
a couple of planets away.

Books give you a sweet taste of the bone,
I reckon, but marrow's another matter.

FOUNTAIN

Ham biscuit makes a body thirsty
so by the time we get to where
the music is, Daddy starts
hunting for a fountain. He
asks a girl handing out
signs. She points to
a bunch of people
across the way.
Colored and
white, all
mixed up.
Turns out
they are drinking from
little   bitty   fountains
on the side of a water truck.
All drinking
side   by   side.

Daddy has me by the hand.
We're almost there when I stop.
"What's wrong, sugar?" he asks,
bending down to me. "Where's
the line for us?" I ask him.
Daddy lifts me straight up
so we're face to face.
"They're *all* for us, Ruby May,"
he tells me. "That's what this
is about."
               I still feel kinda
scared, standing behind a big girl
with blond braids. But after
she gets her drink, I say,
"My   turn   now."

A. Philip Randolph

The gentleman loves the Marchers,
The Marchers love the street
Where heads and hands in heartland
Are meant to follow feet.

The gentleman loves the preacher
Whose wonder-thunder sound
Reverberates on hallowed
And on unhallowed ground.

The people love the gentleman
Whose presence parts the sea
Where white and rugged breakers
Batter equality.

ANNIE ROSS, 19
SPELMAN COLLEGE FOR WOMEN
ATLANTA, GEORGIA

UP CLOSE

At the Monument, somehow our handful
gets wedged near the front close to the platform
where Peter, Paul, and Mary are singing. I stand
right behind a redheaded boy with neck freckles.
I am trying to listen to their song full of questions
but the boy's hair is a color you wouldn't think
a head could make, and he is double-crowned
to boot. Cow-licked to one side. I can smell his
neck. You know how it is in a crowd. Maybe
you don't know, though, how strange it is
for a *colored* girl to stand nose-to-neck with
a freckledy white boy.

                In my head, my mama
is saying, *Step back, Annie! Who do you think
you are?* Before she signed the permission
for me to come on this trip, Mama made
me promise to watch myself, not be loud, not
rile anybody up. *Don't trouble Trouble* is how
she put it.

        But I'm just standing here, Mama,
I want to tell her. I'm just one person in this

46

crowd and that white boy is just another.
Dr. Hobbs believes we can change things.
Probably everybody here believes that. Why
else show up? I guess *everybody* includes me,
Mama. Maybe I just joined the March.

Emma Wallace, 23
Farm Hand
Seymour, Iowa

The U.S. of Anywhere But Home

There, on an urban pasture, more people stood
and swayed than Seymour had yellowing tallboys—
tens of thousands, hand-to-hand and heart-to-heart.

To mark my modest arrival from Jiggety Clop,
a man wearing a bumper sticker across his back—
Jim Crow Must Go—said, "Welcome, Marcher.
Hear that sound? Why, that's Odetta singing
harmony to harmony."

        My mouth crocodiled open
but nothing came out, and for the next hour,
all I did was pick my jaw up off the grass.
I couldn't wait to tell Pa I'd landed on Jupiter.
Somehow, his greenhorn girl—$32 to her name,
plus a tiny "Jobs Now!" flag on a stick—found
a payphone. Jabbering like a jaybird, I described
everything and everyone that was not home,
and how we were all overcoming. Pa listened
patiently—he always had—probably imagining
what he was expecting: his daughter, adrift in
the world for the first time. What he also heard
was his young filly bolt from her tether, about
to outrun the wind and the odds and the field.

ME, TOO

You come on that Freedom Train?
I did. Got on in Beaufort, South Carolina.
Never been on a train before.
Never been out of Jasper County
till I took the bus up to Beaufort.

My neighbor asked wasn't I scared.
I told her I was about to be, but then
I looked in the mirror and my mama's eyes
looked back, and I heard her voice, clear
and sure as when she was alive:
"Cleo, if your grandbabies are ever going
*any*where, you better get to that March."

So I put on my hat and finished packing.
Rode all night. Found the crowd. What
you can see is huge, but there's another
crowd, much bigger: the people we come
from and come *for*. I'm a family by
myself, standing on this grass, saying
"Equal means me, too."

CREED (SONG)

I am not the you of you
And you are not the me of me
But we're here in solidarity—
Brothers, sisters: one (one one one)
Brothers, sisters: One.

We live in different colored skin,
Kin to different colored kin
But it's one march we're marching in
For freedom to be won (won won won)
Brothers, sisters: One.

One country gave us birth.
One birthright gives us worth.
We must stand equal on the earth
For justice to be done (done done)
For freedom to be won (won won won)
Brothers, sisters: One.

LESSONS

"Name's David Boyd"—the words were directed at me, despite my looking as goofy as a mayfly. "This is the best first time to be in DC!" Best *first* time? Was I really that obvious? True, I was struck by how many Negroes wore suits, ties, and dresses, especially in beastly hot weather. So me in overalls might have been a clue that I was the new bird just flown in from south of West Nowhere.

Mr. Boyd introduced his wife, Sherry. "Here you go," she said, cool as ice cream, "put this on your finger. It's a '**LET FREEDOM RING**.'" Which didn't seem at all corny, but the three of us laughed anyway, and the Boyds turned to the next Judy-come-lately.

Well, there was Lesson #1: You didn't have to approach these strangers; they came right on up to you, happy as dragonflies diving for gnats on a farm pond.

Still, I felt it was my turn, so I sailed into a trio of Negro volunteers, stuck all over with stickers and pins. "Name's Emma Wallace. Don't you think this is just the best first time to be in DC?" I repeated. They nodded politely and were kind enough to wait until after I had stepped away to roll their eyes.

I was getting the hang of it, though. Miss Intrepid soldiered on with a few more shameless howdy-dos until Lesson #2 intervened: Remember why you're here. Every person of every color was riveted by speeches that could wake Harriet Tubman. I was as stirred by John Lewis's fluency and fire as by Dr. King's dream and benediction.

And the day swelled to keep faith with its promise of distressing the assured and assuring the distressed.

Tina's Got To . . .

Cody Howard, 28
Car Wash Employee
and Tina Greene, 26
Hairdresser
Anacostia, Washington, DC

conk my hair,
says Cody

find her cat-eye
sunglasses

wash her
beatnik pants

put on her pearl
lipstick

buy me the latest
Ray Charles

open up the
Beauty Shoppe

and besides,
says Cody

it's too hot to be
out marching

Tina doesn't
want to go anyhow

isn't that right, Tina . . .
Tina? *Tina!*

where'd she go?

PIGS ARE FLYIN' (SONG)

Stevie Hatcher, 23, Folk Singer
Kenton, Ohio

I write folk songs to be spoken
Softly by a child of change.
Who cares if politicians think I'm strange?
That's the truth. But truth is fiction,
Often running neck and neck.
Someone's dealing from the bottom of the deck.

What they're sellin', no one's buyin'.
Say we're equal? Hey, you're lyin',
Like that whopper, pigs are flyin'.

Went to high school at Suspicious,
Where I specialized in Doubt,
So I may not have it all quite figured out.
Still, pale pilgrim, look around you,
See how all the Rules are bent?
Yeah, you owe it to the Ruling Establishment.
But today's another story
Told by Promise to Desire
And a multitude consumed with quiet fire.

When you greet a brother pilgrim,
You discover that your hand
Goes electric knowing what you understand.
So you came to see the masses,
Yet you stayed to see the show

You'll remember till they shovel summer snow.
Who arrived a doubtful witness
Will depart as someone who
Heard the message: civil rights are overdue.

That's the truth, there's no denyin',
And the March goes on defyin'
Folks who tell you pigs are flyin'.

ONE-EYED DOLL

Shirley Pearl, 6
First Grader
Elkins, West Virginia

"Mama, I lost my one-eyed doll."
   "*Shhh*, that angel voice is Marian Anderson's."

"But she was in my satchel, and now she's gone."
   "Hush! Blessed Rosa Parks will hear you."

"Maybe she fell out, Mama. Back by that long pool."
   "*Shirl!* A. Philip Randolph is about to speak."

"Lippy Randolph? That brat in my class? Maybe he took it."
   "Lordie, what is all the fuss? That doll's seen better days."

"You'd be in a tizzy, too, if it was *your* doll, Mama!"
   "Tell me, how am I supposed to hear Miss Mahalia
   singing like the bluebird choir? Flapping your gums
   about some no-eyed doll!"

"*One*-eyed, Mama. A green marble."

Anthem for Rosa Parks

She finished up her job at Montgomery Fair,
mending women's clothes for little pay,
the day that came to redefine our lives,
otherwise ordinary in every way.
At six o'clock, she caught the bus for home.
What happened next? For some, original sin.
Was she tired? She said, "The only tired
I was, was tired of giving in."

When J. P. Blake
told her to take
a seat in back—the colored kind,
she thought, *No sir,*
no, I prefer
not moving till you're colorblind.

Blake called police,
"Disturbed the peace!"
They hauled her off to city jail.
The incident,
nonviolent,
took on a superhuman scale.

A woman with the strength to bend the bars
and slip beyond this prejudice-built cage
held up the Book of Tears and Misery
and found the fortitude to burn a page.

Stand up, stand up so everyone can see
the seamstress who restitched the USA.
By sitting down, you stood up to be free:
To Rosa Parks, our aristocracy.

Other Voices

You may think only people
and signs speak—
End Segregated Rules for Public Schools
We Demand Voting Rights Now
AFL-CIO for Full Employment

but listen to staplers
fastening poster board to sticks
Together is better, Together we'll get there

Hear the integrated fountains
Water of life, Flowing for all

and the podium
I await the laying on of hands

and the hot dog stand
Feeding the future, Making change

and the badges pinned over
a quarter of a million hearts
Now   Now   Now   Now

Mr. Ravizee

Sharecropper, 47
Nelson County, Kentucky

Nobody is nobody, that's what I say.
Been treated like a dog, worked like a mule.
We're here for jobs, votes, a better day.

Don't tell me to stick to the old way,
just keep quiet, follow Jim Crow's rule.
Nobody is nobody, that's what I say.

Fair housing, full employment, equal pay.
No more used-up books in run-down schools.
We claim our right. We demand a better day.

Tell the mayors, the governors, tell JFK
we won't be stopped. We're not their fools.
Nobody is nobody. That's what I say.

Together *we the people* are here to stay
in the streets. Passive resistance, our tool
for changing laws to bring our better day.

Up front, they call for action, sing and pray.
Out here, we cool our feet in Lincoln's pool,
feet that will carry us to that better day.
We're all somebody. That's what we say.

COMMITMENT BOUND IN JOY

Eric Blair, 37
Journalist
Peru, Illinois

Imagining a magic rendezvous,
I do not have a moment of regret
at hightailing it to DC from Peru.

My editor's assignment is to get
"the human side of history—one on one.
A front page that our readers won't forget!"

When I see buses lining Washington,
it seems as if I levitated here
until an old man pokes me: "Wake up, son."

I do! And witness freedom in the air:
The Marchers stepping to their last resort.
Commitment bound in joy in one town square!

I'll pack their dignity in my report,
a piece that paints the atmosphere, the *feel*
of pride in hauling bigotry to court.

A little self-reflection will reveal
the mission on the Mall, its mass appeal—
a shattered nation learning how to heal.

ANNIE ROSS, 19
SPELMAN COLLEGE FOR WOMEN
ATLANTA, GEORGIA

MOVING

*(BEFORE THE OFFICIAL NOON STARTING TIME,
THE MARCH BEGINS ON ITS OWN)*

We are moving now—a sea of people, a swarm of bees.
I'm singing *Woke up this morning with my mind   stayed on
freedom* and can feel my voice behind my breastbone but
I can't hear it. So many singers! At the Monument, the
crowd divides and curls back, my wing turning down
Independence Avenue, sun hot through thinning leaves,
and now the song is *We shall not, we shall not be moved.*
I feel strength I know is not mine any more than this
mighty voice is mine, and all of a sudden *deep in my heart*
I know we are being carried, being sung. Steadfast going
forward—a woman ahead in a wheelchair, a man behind
with a baby on his back.

POLLY

Out of this anonymous hot universe
sprang Polly Hazlett, both of us
negotiating melting snow cones:
two Iowaywards who'd grown up
less than seventy miles apart.

A first-year schoolteacher
from Des Moines, Polly concealed a
worldly-wise sophistication. Shy
and unassuming, she wore her
learning lightly with sentences
that trotted and cantered along
in keeping with the day's occasion.

Participating in the bubble-up
of history, we spent the start
of what I knew then would be
a lifelong friendship, prouder
of being there on that solid
ground than of anything
in our young lives.

RIDING HIGH

When the crowd finally starts to move, I ride
on my daddy's shoulders, and I can see what looks
like all the people in the world, marching and singing
together *Ain't gonna let nobody turn me 'round   turn
me 'round   turn me 'round . . .*   I can feel the song
through my daddy's headbone. He has a big voice
and springy black hair. I like to press it down and watch
it jump back. Daddy holds my feet, his hard hands over
my tennis shoes. In between songs and chants he calls
out, "You okay up there, baby?" "Lovin' life," I answer,
because that's what my grandma said till the day she died.
"How you doing, Mama?" Daddy'd ask her and she'd say,
"Clarence, son, I'm just lovin' life." Daddy laughs at those
words out of my mouth. In my heart, where Mama says
you talk to Jesus, I tell Grandma, *Maybe life loves us back.*

RAYMOND JARVIS, 25
B.A. DEGREE IN BUSINESS ADMINISTRATION
OUT-OF-WORK STORE CLERK
AMARILLO, TEXAS

FIRST IMPRESSIONS

At the Lincoln Monument,
a sparrow twinkles
in the corner of his eye,
just like my granddaddy's
eye would twinkle seeing me
on tiptoes next to Grandma,
clotheslining the laundry.
Now here comes foolish me,
tearing up when I first see
honest Abe, deep in thought,
in his Georgia marble suit.

Two words for this unstoppable
crowd that could fill five football
stadiums: *unshakable* and *peaceful*.
All right, I'll add *contagious*!
In lockstep to the chant, "Jobs,
Freedom, Equality," I focus
to fight on, my legs pounding
like pistons over somebody's
white idea of paradise.

I overhear a preacher—a bear
of a man—tell his Negro-
and-white parish of seven:
"If you keep track of all
the wrongs ever done to you,
do it with a pencil *and* an eraser."
Good advice. I take up my own
sheet of paper and title it,
"In Praise of the Warriors
Who Make Us See the Very
Best in Ourselves."

So far, it's a short list.

Raymond Jarvis, 25
B.A. Degree in Business Administration
Out-of-Work Store Clerk
Amarillo, Texas

THE ONE AND ONLY MALCOLM X

Who never knows doubt
Who trades on talk with the down-and-out
Who refuses to accept mere tolerance
Who refuses to tolerate mere acceptance
Who comes to what he calls the "Farce on Washington,"
	but only to watch
Who is a Washington monument of contempt
Who retches at hypocrisy
Who ridicules Uncle Toms
Who knows
And knows he knows
That we will still be marching in 2063,
One hundred years from now

Dan Cantrell, 16
Rabun County High School Junior
Dillard, Georgia

Make a New Tomorrow

I was lucky enough to get one of those
cheese sandwiches that came in a box
and after we'd marched from George to Abe
—that's how I thought of it—I sat down
on the grass to eat. A colored girl named
Mavis sat beside me to do the same. She
had a cheese sandwich, too. Since the sound
system was fuzzy right there, we started

talking. She was from Florida, had
come on the Freedom Train. I told her
about Judy Gilley and we laughed so hard
bread crumbs flew out of my mouth. We'd
been talking maybe ten minutes, having
a blast, when all of a sudden she froze.
No smile. No light in her eyes. "What's wrong?"
I asked. She shook her head, her eyes wide,
then got it out. "If we sat together like this
back home, tomorrow I could be dead."

Renée Newsome, 15
Coolidge High School Sophomore
Washington, DC

DADDY CALLS

I let my bare feet dangle
  in the Reflecting Pool.
Couldn't recall ever feeling
  anything so cool.

I flipped a buffalo nickel
  end over end.
Sorry, pool, I've got no more
  buffaloes to spend.

Tossed it out in the middle,
  thirty inches deep—
Pool has got its very own
  buffalo to keep.

Watched my Daddy watching
  folks sashaying by.
Heard my Daddy calling
  my Daddy's solemn cry:

"Renée, we're almost there.
  Oh Lord, it won't be long."
Didn't know my Daddy
  could be so Daddy-wrong.

Dan Cantrell, 16
Rabun County High School Junior
Dillard, Georgia

I Get It

Hot as it was, my
spine was ice when Mavis stood
said Sorry, walked off.

I felt sick. Stupid.
Shamed. I got up, made my way
to shade trees. Climbed one.

A New World

There's helicopters above us all
the time. Seems like they hover
lower when we pour out one end
of the Mall, march up streets on
either side, and come back in
to face Lincoln. To whoever's up
there we must look like a band
on the field at halftime or a pair
of big old snakes doing some dance.
I like snakes myself. Keep down
rats. Protect your corncrib.

I am waiting to use the facility,
waiting in the same line as white
folks, which is just about unbelievable,
when a college girl in front of me
tells her friend she has never had
to resort to such as this before, and
she's been trying all day not to go.
Well, honey, I want to say, it's
a new world for both of us.

TURN

Aki Kimura, 46
Printer
San Jose, California

I'm neither black nor white but it's my March
too. My March because in Los Angeles
in the spring of 1942, I walked out of
an art class, out of my life, and onto
a bus, bound for an internment
camp with all my family.
Japanese-American
threat was how
they saw us:
120,000
folks
about half
the number
who fill this
mile-long Mall.
Listen. Our country
takes very wrong turns
and counts on you and me
to set it right. In most countries
citizens can't do that, but here it's
our job—to steer toward justice together.

RENÉE NEWSOME, 15
COOLIDGE HIGH SCHOOL SOPHOMORE
WASHINGTON, DC

WHERE'S LANGSTON?

I admit it.
I'm not ready
for the Rev. Dr.
Martin Luther King Jr.
I see him for about five
seconds over a million
heads turtling up to the front.
Oh, I know every girl
at Coolidge High idolizes him.
But what this crowd needs
is the spark of Langston
Hughes. Now there's a poet
who can catch the fire
and spread the flame.

JOAN BAEZ
found in her autobiography,
And a Voice to Sing With

In the blistering sun,
facing the original
rainbow coalition,
I led 350,000 people
in "We Shall Overcome,"
and I was near my beloved
Dr. King when he put aside
his prepared speech and let
the breath of God thunder
through him, and up over
my head I saw freedom,
and all around me
I heard it ring.

Ballad for Martin Luther King Jr.

Bev Rockwell, 62
Folk Singer/Street Poet
Richmond, Kentucky

Ten thousands join ten thousands
Without goading police.
The singers sing, their anthems ring,
The speakers speak their peace.

Around the world astonishment—
The ceremonies heard
Or seen on every continent,
And still to come: the Word.

Spectators waving handkerchiefs,
Small children, hearts to seize,
Will tell it taller years from now,
Grandchildren at their knees.

Blue sunshine worships afternoon,
No cloud will dare to rain
For in his jacket, mercy,
And in his pocket, pain.

Equality his brother
And sisterhood his pride
Meet common sense, nonviolence,
The means he's deified.

The crowd's a crush, but it falls hush—
The Reverend takes the stage.
George Washington spreads out the book,
Abe Lincoln turns the page.

He reads his notes religiously—
An old familiar theme.
"But please, Martin," Mahalia yells,
"Tell 'em about the dream!"

And first he puts away his speech
Then sweeps away the crowd:
The memory of his remarks
Peals like a thundercloud.

"The content of our character"
Personifies a sage.
One day in 1963
Belongs to every age.

CORETTA SCOTT KING

There was a thread on the back of his jacket
and I didn't see it till he stood to speak
a white thread on the black expanse of his back.

I'll get it later, I thought, as he drew his first
words' breath. But *Later* was another world.

American Dream

I was about give out
Wished I'd not worn the good blue shoes
cast off by Mrs. Rufus I clean for
but my old ones that stretch where the bunion is.

I was about to drag my dogs
back to that bus
and drink sweet tea
from the Thermos bottle
when the Rev. Dr. King took the stand

Took our used-up air
into his deep chest
up close to his heart
and gave out the news
we'd come for:

Now is the time to make justice
a reality for all of God's children. . . .

meaning me
and my husband
and Daniel and Jessie Lee—
all my kin as sure
as those Kennedy kids,

me from Pralltown
with sprung chairs
and floors about scrubbed through

and feet blistered in somebody else's shoes.

RENÉE NEWSOME, 15
COOLIDGE HIGH SCHOOL SOPHOMORE
WASHINGTON, DC

STUNNED

The sound rumbling out
of the microphone is foreign
somehow: words punching
like a heavyweight then
pirouetting like a ballerina.

Someone coughs, someone
sighs. It is all they can do,
all anyone can do.

As if he's instructing birds,
the Rev. Dr. Martin Luther King Jr.
watches his words flutter up
and drop a blessing of hallelujah-
amen grace notes across the nation.

When he says he has a dream,
I have one too, my dream
blinking on and off like neon
in windows on Georgia Avenue.
My tightrope-wire nerves jolt
and jangle, ripple and trip, and
I know that I will no longer look
back at who it was I was, but
keep my eyes fixed ahead
on who I am becoming.

DAN CANTRELL, 16
RABUN COUNTY HIGH SCHOOL JUNIOR
DILLARD, GEORGIA

TREE

That's why
I was up there when
Roy Wilkins, head of the NAACP,
said, "I want to hear a yell and a thunder
from those people out there under the trees
. . . there's even one *in* the trees." I yelled my fool
head off, hollered so hard I almost lost my balance
in that late-August maple. Me, a white boy, perched
in the crown of that tree above so many Negroes whose
ancestors, whose kin, had been hung from one. I climbed to
have something to hold on to and wound up being caught by
cameras, even the helicopter's. Never mind. Never mind that I
was in DC as much to march away from the bonds of my own
family as to free those our country rose on the backs of. I had
no clue. It was Mavis I was yelling for, outraged at the truth
in the fear that drove her away. It doesn't matter
that I was yelling for a girl and not for her
people, for all of us.
Whatever
got me
out on
that
limb,
served.

ANNIE ROSS, 19
SPELMAN COLLEGE FOR WOMEN
ATLANTA, GEORGIA

WHAT HAPPENED TO MY HEART

By the time we get to the Lincoln Memorial,
we are starving. Hattie spots a hot dog stand,
and we snake over and join the line. The wait
is long and it costs too much, but that scalded
dog slathered with mustard is one of the tastiest
meals I've ever had. Mouth full, I say, We're
having the world's biggest picnic. The most
colorful, too. And not a sign of that *Trouble*
Mama's so scared of.

        Then the Freedom Singers
climb up on the stage. We're far back, and I'm
not that interested. Oh, I know about them. Kids
like me, they've been singing around the country,
raising hope and money. One of them even went
to Spelman. I know their first song, "This Little
Light of Mine," too, but they give it new words:
All in the street I'm gonna let it shine
All in the jailhouse   I'm gonna let it shine—
and when the stream of those words, those
harmonies, braided tight as my mama used to do

my hair, pours into me, I am gone. I shout, I cry,
I wail into that blue sky. I let loose a thing
I didn't know was in me—the part that had never
been free, their singing lets it out. I sing
with them in a voice I've never heard before.
It's huge and it's mine and my mama's
and grandmama's. My light and it is shining.
And in that moment, I fall in love
with what I have to do: Live this work.
Sing what's true. Figure out how.

WHAT COMES NEXT

My mama always told me to watch out for the Sight.
Her mama had it and she doesn't and it likes to skip down
the line. I never thought much about it to tell you the truth.
I was too busy growing up, falling in love, and trying to change
the world. That's how I got to the March. So here I am, clothed
in my best dress and righteousness, standing two Marchers back
from the pool. My head is sweaty and the long day has lowered
my shoulders. But then the Rev. Dr. King speaks and we are
lifted on the wings of his voice. That is when the thing
Mama warned me about happens. Color drains from all
I see except that pool, and it is one long street of blood.

RAYMOND JARVIS, 25
B.A. DEGREE IN BUSINESS ADMINISTRATION
OUT-OF-WORK STORE CLERK
AMARILLO, TEXAS

QUESTIONS I ASK MYSELF ON THE BUS RIDE HOME

What should I do? My temper's set on rage.
What will I be if fires cease to burn?
What can I give if what I bring is hate?
What can I learn from those who never learn?

Who owns the wealth, stealthily white-endowed?
Who runs a world where we are not allowed?
Who sees the good, and never will address
Seasons of loss and painful bitterness?

Who speaks of peace, but wants to bellow war?
Who speaks of love, but carries on the fraud
That fellowship and brotherhood are served
Through spiteful acts of vengefulness, by God?

DARRYL

When we get back home, who's standing there?
"Figures," says Grandma, "he's combing his hair."

Darryl glares at me. "Where've you been, Renée?
Marching? Is that how you wasted your day?"

Daddy says, "Listen here. . . ," but he thinks twice,
too happy today to give him Darryl-advice.

A cloud of embarrassment. No one moves
till Grandma tells Darryl she disapproves:

"I don't allow that kind of attitude."
He hollers back sass that is downright rude.

I shout after him as he struts away,
"I'm not the Renée I was yesterday."

I Wasn't There

I was old enough to go.
I was in college.
I wasn't there
because I didn't
see a problem.
Being from Georgia,
what they called
separate but equal
was working fine for me.

Everybody has their place
was what I was taught.
There's the foot
of the leg of the table,
there's the leg that holds the table up,
there's the table top
there's the farmers who grow the food
and the pickers who harvest it
and the grocers who sell it
and the women who shop
and cook and serve

and then there's those of us
who get to eat.

I was blind as that table.
I was dumb as any floor it could have stood on

till white men bombed the Birmingham church
eighteen days after the March.

One of the four girls killed
was my sister Lynna's age—
Lynna, who had gone to church
that same morning
just fifty-six miles away.

Only a lack
of pigment in her skin
kept Lynna alive
kept my mother from wailing
kept me from raging
through the streets.

That night
I felt the call
of Dr. King's dream

and I knew

the life I counted on
was standing in its way.

I knelt down
but I didn't have a prayer.

I'd been baptized
in lies.

RAYMOND JARVIS, 25
B.A. DEGREE IN BUSINESS ADMINISTRATION
OUT-OF-WORK STORE CLERK
AMARILLO, TEXAS

ANSWERS

The March
>   is the end of the beginning—
>   or the beginning, not the end.

The March
>   is the critical first inning
>   that nasty weather might suspend.

The March
>   delights every make-believer,
>   of which, no, I was never one.

The March—
>   will Americans catch the fever
>   that cries "For All or None"?

DEAR RENÉE

Here's a poem I wrote
about what happened
to us three short summers
ago, remember?

August-toasted 83°
was like icebox frost
on slow burn to me.
If you never got

the chilly-bumps
in summer, this was
it. Whites hung on
Negroes, both hung

on the slip edge of
wonder. Speechifying
to stir Mr. Lincoln's
envy nicked every

curve of every nerve.
As angels hummed,
strumming heaven's
guitars, Mahalia

and her sweet
singers nearly broke
my heart and the soul
sound barrier—

a glorious ending.
But folks inching on
home stopped short—
a Poet took the stage.

Rev. King's voice blew
it in—the crystal door
of the white mansion—
ka-blam! Write it down,

Precious. Go ahead,
write it down now,
circle it, dog-ear
the page—the date,

August 28, 1963—
the day an ebony
rainbow spelled out
P R O M I S E

Love and vinegar,
Your Grandma Rascal

AUGUST 28, 2013

Polly, my always-welcome visitor, clinks my glass.
"A lemonade toast to fifty years!" On the back porch
swing, quartering navel oranges, she gives me a look
I've known since the back of forever. "Emma," she says,
"some 18,000 days ago, we were two little scythes
helping sweep the Earth off its orbit. Sure,
there's a Supreme Court of obstacles blacks have yet
to overcome. But think of the fertile seeds we helped
plant back then and how they've grown."

A lone cloud hurries off to Wisconsin. Stars tumble down
so close we might touch them. "The March was courage
outright, Polly. Courage by Dr. King and every soul-
searcher there. Have you ever been a part of anything
more galvanizing?"

We reminisce, adding heavy dollops of Iowa gossip
into the mix—jobs, neighbors, husbands, children,
in-laws, and whatnot. Delighting in the company of
our alter-egos, we settle back on the swing and name
the stars, letting the billion-acre sky swallow us whole.

RENÉE NEWSOME-WADE, 67
D.ED., HEAD OF SPECIAL EDUCATION
DISTRICT OF COLUMBIA PUBLIC SCHOOLS
WASHINGTON, DC

AT GRANDMA RASCAL'S GRAVE, JANUARY 19, 2015

Praise the Lord, it's Martin Luther King Jr. Day!
Can you believe it? Children even get off school.
I brought Imani and Raj along to say *hey* to their
Great-Great-Grandma Rascal. Imani says you're
not really in the ground, that you must be up
in heaven with God, tickling Him silly.

I kept my Rascal promise: To share with all our
Newsome, Reese, and Wade relatives my wet-hankie
memories of the spitfire miracle that was you.

Uh, excuse me a minute, Grandma. . . . *Raj, Imani!*
Kindly move away from that open burial plot.
Come pay your respects. Quietly, please.

You were right, dear: We have overcome. Those
whites-only, fast-lane freeways—one-lane, potholed
for blacks—have opened up . . . mostly. We used
to hit every red light on Freedom Road. Now they

blink caution going green. So we are moving slowly
through heavy traffic.

No one will forget your Dr. King–sized courage
and ornery love. I'll come visit again when my
Rascal cup needs a refill. Till then, keep teasing
the angels, and let your spirit always surround
the grateful family you founded. Your bones
are buried deep, but it's nothing like the hole
you left in our hearts.

Now Imani, Raj, what would you like to say to Grandma Rascal?

Amen. Amen.

LAST IMPRESSIONS

black without white
is
a moonless
night
empty
as
a life
of
endlessly
falling
snow
is
white without black

A GUIDE to the VOICES

In 1963 at the March on Washington for Jobs and Freedom, reporters tried to capture the jumble of emotions on display. Even the most eager among them could not have hoped to interview more than a handful of the 250,000 laughing, waving, singing, praying souls.

Journalists and historians published many of these personal stories. Ordinary citizens, witnesses to that time, told others. Taken as a whole, these tales reflect the profound and life-changing experiences of the people who were there.

Who wouldn't have been transported by the Rev. Dr. Martin Luther King Jr.'s spellbinding "I Have a Dream" speech? Or by seeing the diminutive giant Rosa Parks? Or by linking arms with strangers—black and white—to sing the incandescent anthem, "We Shall Overcome"?

But prose writers and memoirists need not have the field all to themselves. Poets have their own way of recreating events. How? Books, films, and music are tickets to ride. They provide the research fuel to get you there. By what sort of conveyance? you ask. The best that money can't buy: the poet's imagination.

Voices from the March on Washington is not a book designed to compete with encyclopedia entries, which may be rich in detail but emotionally empty. Our objective, through poetry, was to imagine the testimony of people who were there. We wanted to envision their passions, the intensity of knowing and *feeling* that they were present at a pivotal moment in their nation's history and their own—one that took them entirely beyond themselves. We painted ordinary citizens doing one quite extraordinary thing—marching for jobs and freedom for the disenfranchised and the dispossessed.

Our own experiences, of course, fed our fellow feeling and sense of urgency in the task. Both of us came of age in the heyday of the civil rights movement. One of us was initiated in local marches—against discrimination and union-busting in the early and mid-1960s in Gary, and then Bloomington, Indiana. The other, a high school freshman in 1963, became an activist in college, picketing the segregated barbershop and volunteering in the free preschool program. Two states apart, we both marched against the Vietnam War.

Together we wanted to revisit the March, which Dr. King called "the greatest demonstration for freedom in the history of our nation." Where did the Marchers and their courage come from? Why did they come? How did they remain peaceful, despite the fervor in their hearts and the swelter of the day?

In light of our current atmosphere of political polarization, with an ever-widening gap between rich and poor, the unity of vision and purpose the Marchers enacted is nothing short of astounding.

The diversity of humanity that day could best be seen, we decided, by presenting an equally diverse patchwork of voices: famous dignitaries on stage along with imaginary characters in the crowd. Together they packed—*imagine!*—the entire distance between the Lincoln Memorial and the Washington Monument on a most memorable day in American history: August 28, 1963.

These are the stories told in the Marchers' own words . . . well, in our words. We hope you enjoy these fictional citizens and their memories as much as we enjoyed creating them.

—*JPL* (with *GEL*)

HISTORICAL VOICES

The "Big Six"—the men who organized and led the March on Washington for Jobs and Freedom:

1. **Dr. Martin Luther King Jr.** (1929–1968, assassinated): president of the Southern Christian Leadership Conference (1957–1968), pastor, activist, humanitarian, and recipient of the Nobel Peace Prize.

2. **A. Philip Randolph** (1889–1979): founder of the Brotherhood of Sleeping Car Porters in 1925, co-founder (with Roy Wilkins and Arnold Aronson) of the Leadership Conference on Civil Rights in 1950, socialist, and labor activist.

3. **James Farmer** (1920–1999): founder of Congress of Racial Equality (CORE).

4. **Roy Wilkins** (1901–1981): executive director of the NAACP (1955–1977).

5. **John Lewis** (1940–): then chairman of the Student Nonviolent Coordinating Committee (SNCC); now a member of the US House of Representatives (1986 to the present).

6. **Whitney Moore Young Jr.** (1921–1971): head of the National Urban League (1961–1971).

A seventh man, **Bayard Rustin** (1912–1987), the chief organizer of the March, deserves special mention. Rustin was a civil rights activist and proponent of pacifism and gay rights. Prejudice against gays would begin to be addressed nationally by the end of the decade.

Six "**Negro Women Fighters for Freedom**" were listed on the program and seated on the platform at the March, but only one—**Daisy Bates**—was allowed to speak. In addition, they were not allowed to march with the Big Six and the media but were routed down Independence Avenue instead. While the civil rights movement called for an end to institutionalized racism, it was blind to issues of sexism, another ubiquitous form of discrimination that the feminist movement would soon take up.

OTHER NOTABLES WHOSE NAMES APPEAR IN THE BOOK

(Names in **BOLD** indicate people who attended the March.)

Henry "Hank" Aaron (1934–): major league baseball star.

Muhammad Ali (1942–2016): professional boxer, heavyweight champion, and social activist.

Marian Anderson (1897–1993): contralto singer. She was the first African American singer to perform at the White House and at the Metropolitan Opera in New York City.

Joan Baez (1941–): pacifist, folk singer, songwriter, and activist.

Daisy Bates (1914–1999): civil rights activist, publisher, and journalist. Head of the Arkansas NAACP (1952–1961), she shepherded the Little Rock Nine and risked her life to demand the desegregation of Little Rock Central High School in 1957. The only woman allowed to speak at the March, Bates spoke in place of Myrlie Evers.

Diane Nash Bevel (1938–): civil rights activist. She led the campaign to desegregate Nashville lunch counters, helped found the Student Nonviolent Coordinating Committee (SNCC), and advocated the continuation of the Freedom Rides when violence threatened to halt them. The Rev. Dr. Martin Luther King Jr. called her "the driving spirit in the nonviolent assault on segregation at lunch counters."

Brooklyn brethren: The New York chapter of CORE organized a 237-mile trip on foot from Brooklyn to the March for some of its members. It took nearly two weeks. Anna Arnold Hedgeman, a March committee member, and the other walkers carried signs that read: "We March from New York City for Freedom."

Ray Charles (1930–2004): American singer and songwriter; a pioneer of soul music, who also had country and pop music hits.

Jim Crow: Jim Crow was not actually a person. The Jim Crow laws were named after a character created by the white entertainer Thomas Dartmouth Rice and performed in the 1830s and 1840s. Rice performed in blackface, and his hateful caricature lived on in American entertainments called minstrel shows. Jim Crow laws legalized segregation in the majority of American states from the 1870s until the Civil Rights Act of 1964, restricting where blacks could live, work, and go to school, and denying them service in white-owned restaurants. Public facilities such as waiting rooms in bus and train stations, restrooms, and water fountains were all segregated, and those provided for blacks were often filthy. In addition, blacks had no recourse to change Jim Crow laws since they were also denied the right to vote. They lived under a form of domestic terrorism, knowing that, if they challenged this system in any way, their property, their jobs, their very lives could be taken from them. This violence increased as some whites pushed back against the civil rights movement's demand for change. Less than a month after Dr. King told the Marchers about his dream, he gave the eulogy for three of the four young girls killed in the bombing of the 16th Street Baptist Church in Birmingham, Alabama. Just as Jim Crow laws gave whites the best seats on buses and trains, these laws assured whites the best chances in day-to-day living, and in life in general.

Ossie Davis (1917–2005): film, television, and Broadway actor.

Medgar Evers (1925–1963, assassinated): Field Secretary for the NAACP in Mississippi, best known for his efforts to overturn segregation at the University of Mississippi.

Myrlie Evers (1933–): civil rights activist, journalist, and chair of the NAACP (1995–1998). She continued her work as an activist even after her house was fire-bombed and her husband, Medgar Evers, was assassinated. Her name appeared on the program to speak at the March, but she was forced to decline due to her commitment to address the National Convention of Negro Elks in Boston, Massachusetts.

Jay Hardon (dates unknown): Mr. Hardon rode his bicycle 750 miles from Dayton, Ohio, to get to the March in Washington. He was 82.

Charlton Heston (1923–2008): Hollywood actor, who starred in *Ben Hur* and *The Ten Commandments*.

Lena Horne (1917–2010): singer, actress, and civil rights activist.

Langston Hughes (1902–1967): poet, novelist, playwright, and civil rights activist.

Charlie Jackson (1924–1999): detective from Jersey City, New Jersey. Jackson was one of many out-of-town police officers who volunteered to help the Washington Police Department guard Dr. King. In the poem "M," he describes the day's events. Mr. Jackson stood directly behind Dr. King in many famous photographs. During the speech, he told his son later, he saw two clouds form a cross, which he took as "a sign from God" because Dr. King's words were so powerful.

Mahalia Jackson (1911–1972): gospel singer who performed at the March and encouraged Dr. King to depart from his prepared remarks and "tell 'em about the dream."

John F. Kennedy (1917–1963, assassinated): 35th US president (1961–1963). On June 11, 1963, President Kennedy called for civil rights legislation to end segregation and protect the right to vote. This legislation—the Civil Rights Act of 1964 and the Voting Rights Act of 1965—was passed after his death.

Coretta Scott King (1927–2006): musician, author, civil rights activist, and wife of Rev. Dr. Martin Luther King Jr.

Prince Lee (dates unknown): widow of murdered Mississippi civil rights activist Herbert Lee. In 2010, at age 93, she attended the dedication of a marker in Mississippi to honor her late husband. She had eight children, one of whom said, "I never saw her instill one word of hatefulness in us."

Rosa Parks (1913–2005): seamstress and civil rights activist who, in Montgomery, Alabama, 1955, refused to obey a bus driver's order to give up her seat for a white passenger, launching the Montgomery bus boycott.

Peter, Paul, and Mary: the most popular folk group of the 1960s. Peter Yarrow, Noel Paul Stookey, and Mary Travers sang out for justice in a career that spanned almost fifty years. The song Annie Ross hears them sing in "Up Close" is Bob Dylan's "Blowin' in the Wind." They also sang Pete Seeger and Lee Hays's iconic "If I Had a Hammer." In addition to singing at both ends of the Mall, they sang that morning at Union Station to welcome Marchers arriving by train.

Gloria Richardson (1922–): best known as the cofounder of the Cambridge Nonviolent Action Movement, an organization to desegregate hospitals and schools and implement fair housing in Cambridge, Maryland, in the early 1960s. Richardson was handed a microphone at the March on Washington but only allowed to say "hello."

Jackie Robinson (1919–1972): activist for civil rights and the labor movement. Robinson was the first black baseball player to break the color bar and join a major league baseball team. Dr. King once said that if it weren't for Jackie Robinson, he couldn't have done what he did.

Ledger Smith (dates unknown): a professional roller skater, "Roller Man" Smith left Chicago on August 17, 1963. Watched by the FBI, he skated 685 miles over the course of ten days to join the March.

Harriet Tubman (1820–1913): abolitionist and Union spy during the Civil War, she was perhaps the best-known of the Underground Railroad's "conductors." During a ten-year period, she made nineteen trips to the South and shepherded over 300 slaves to freedom.

Malcolm X (1925–1965, assassinated): Nation of Islam minister, human rights activist, and opponent of the March on Washington.

IMAGINED VOICES

Eric Blair, 37 (journalist, Peru, Illinois)

David and Sherry Boyd, 40 and 37 (volunteers at the March; the "Let Freedom Ring" ring that they give to Emma Wallace is fictional)

Edith and Harry Burlingame, 52 and 54 (newlyweds, Fort Lauderdale, Florida)

Dan Cantrell, 16 (Rabun County High School junior, Dillard, Georgia)

Halley Liza Clemons, 30 (hotel maid, Nashville, Tennessee)

Everett Goodfellow, 64 (WWI veteran and great-grandson of a slave, Mayfair, Washington, DC)

Tina Greene, 26 (hairdresser, Anacostia, Washington, DC)

Stevie Hatcher, 23 (folk singer, Kenton, Ohio)

Myrtle Hill, 60 (high school teacher, Baltimore, Maryland)

Ruby May Hollingsworth, 6 (first grader, Mountain Home, Arkansas)

Cody Howard, 28 (car wash employee, Anacostia, Washington, DC)

Arthur Howe, 8 (third grader, Washington, DC)

Raymond Jarvis, 25 (B.A. degree in business administration and out-of-work store clerk, Amarillo, Texas)

Aki Kimura, 46 (printer, San Jose, California)

Renée Newsome, 15 (Coolidge High School sophomore, Washington, DC)

Shirley Pearl, 6 (first grader, Elkins, West Virginia)

MR. RAVIZEE, 47 (sharecropper, Nelson County, Kentucky)

MARCELLA "GRANDMA RASCAL" REESE, 59 (Renée Newsome's grandmother, Charleston, West Virginia)

BEV ROCKWELL, 62 (folk singer/street poet, Richmond, Kentucky)

ANNIE ROSS, 19 (Spelman College for Women, Atlanta, Georgia)

REBEKAH STODDARD, 25 (Howard University graduate student, Washington, DC)

TY TUCKER AND HIS POLICE PATROL (Washington, DC)

IRENE TURLEY, 38 (professional oboist, New York City, New York)

LORETTA TURNER, 55 (waitress, Oxford, Mississippi)

EMMA WALLACE, 23 (farm hand, Seymour, Iowa)

BIBLIOGRAPHY

Anderson, Jervis. *Bayard Rustin: Troubles I've Seen: A Biography*. New York: HarperCollins, 1997.

Baez, Joan. *And a Voice to Sing With: A Memoir*. New York: Simon & Schuster, 1987.

Bass, Patrick Henry. *Like a Mighty Stream: The March on Washington, August 28, 1963*. Philadelphia: Running Press, 2002.

Branch, Taylor. *The King Years: Historic Moments in the Civil Rights Movement*. New York: Simon & Schuster, 2013.

Branch, Taylor. *Parting the Waters: America in the King Years 1954–63*. New York: Simon & Schuster, 1988.

Branch, Taylor. *Pillar of Fire: America in the King Years 1963–65*. New York: Simon & Schuster, 1999.

Brown, Jim. *Peter, Paul, and Mary: Carry It On: A Musical Legacy.*
Directed by Jim Brown. PBS, Rhino Home Video, 2004. Video.

Euchner, Charles. *Nobody Turn Me Around: A People's History of the
1963 March on Washington.* Boston: Beacon Press, 2011.

To Form a More Perfect Union: Milestones of the Civil Rights Movement.
Directed by Steve Crawford. U.S. Allegiance, Inc., 2005. DVD.

Graves, Kerry A. *I Have a Dream.* Philadelphia: Chelsea Club House,
2004.

Hansen, Drew D. *The Dream: Martin Luther King, Jr., and the Speech
that Inspired a Nation.* New York: Ecco, 2003.

Haskins, James. *The March on Washington.* New York: HarperCollins,
1993.

Jones, Clarence B., and Stuart Connelly. *Behind the Dream: The Making
of the Speech that Transformed a Nation.* New York: Palgrave
Macmillan, 2011.

Jones, William P. *The March on Washington: Jobs, Freedom, and the
Forgotten History of Civil Rights.* New York: W.W. Norton &
Company, 2013.

Kates, Nancy, and Bennett Singer. *Brother Outsider: The Life of Bayard
Rustin.* Directed by Nancy Kates and Bennett Singer. POV, season
15, episode 9. PBS, 2003.

Levine, Daniel. *Bayard Rustin and the Civil Rights Movement.*
Piscataway, NJ: Rutgers University Press, 2000.

Lyon, Danny. *Memories of the Southern Civil Rights Movement.* Chapel
Hill: University of North Carolina Press, 1992.

Martin Luther King: "I Have a Dream." MPI Media Group, 2005. Video.

Reagon, Bernice Johnson. "Witness to Freedom and Song." *The Story.*
American Public Media. September 6, 2011.

Spector, Mark, and Mary Wharton. *Joan Baez: How Sweet the Sound*. American Masters, season 23, episode 7. Directed by Mary Wharton. PBS, 2009. DVD.

"They Come Marching Up Conscience Road." *Life*. September 6, 1963.

Williams, Juan. *A. Philip Randolph: For Jobs and Freedom*. Directed by Dante James. Washington, DC: WETA, 1996.

Williams, Juan. *Eyes on the Prize: America's Civil Rights Years, 1954–1965*. New York: Viking Press, 1987.

Wiliams, Juan. *Eyes on the Prize: America's Civil Rights Years, 1954–1965*. Directed by Henry Hampton, narrated by Julian Bond. PBS, 1987.

WEBSITES*

Martin Luther King, Jr. and the Global Freedom Struggle: March on Washington for Jobs and Freedom.
http://mlk-kpp01.stanford.edu/index.php/encyclopedia/encyclopedia/enc_march_on_washington_for_jobs_and_freedom/.
This site contains a synopsis of the March but also provides important links to individuals, organizations, and events associated with the civil rights movement.

National Museum of African American History and Culture, "The March on Washington."
http://www.youtube.com/watch?v=ZA9TJCV-tks.
In this eighteen-minute film, you will meet many moments visited in *Voices from the March on Washington*: the recruiting truck, the Freedom Singers, the speakers, the signs and fountains, and the young man in the tree.

*Websites active at time of publication

Veterans of the Civil Rights Movement: Images of a People's Movement.
http://www.crmvet.org/images/imgmow.htm.

A Mall view of the day of the March itself with iconic photos of those who were there plus the full text of Dr. King's "I Have a Dream" speech.

BOOKS ON THE MARCH FOR YOUNG READERS

Farris, Christine King. *March On! The Day My Brother Martin Changed the World.* New York: Scholastic Press, 2008.

King, Martin Luther, Jr. *I Have a Dream.* Illustrations by Kadir Nelson. New York: Schwartz & Wade, 2012.

Krull, Kathleen. *What Was the March on Washington?* New York: Grosset & Dunlap, 2013.

Rappaport, Doreen. *Martin's Big Words: The Life of Dr. Martin Luther King, Jr.* New York: Disney-Hyperion, 2007.

INDEX OF POEMS BY TITLE

INDEX OF POEMS BY VOICE